병원에 간 니타

Nita Goes to Hospital

Story by Henriette Barkow

Models and Illustrations by Chris Petty

Korean translation by Yun Young-Min

니타는 록키와 공놀이를 하고 있었어요. "물어와!" 니타는 소리쳤어요. 록키는 뛰어올라 공을 잡으려 했지만, 공은 공원바깥의 도로로 굴러갔어요.
"멈춰! 록키! 멈춰!" 니타는 소리치며 록키를 잡으려고 미쳐 달려오는 무언가를 보지 못했어요.

Nita was playing ball with Rocky. "Catch!" she shouted. Rocky jumped, missed and ran after the ball, out of the park and into the road.
"STOP! ROCKY! STOP!" Nita shouted. She was so busy trying to catch Rocky that she didn't see...

자동차 였어요.

the CAR.

운전사는 힘차게 브레이크를 밟았어요. 끽!~~~
그러나 너무 늦었어요! 쿵! 자동차에 치인
니타는 도로에 쓰러졌어요.

The driver slammed on the brakes. SCREECH! But it was too late! THUD! The car hit Nita and she fell to the ground with a sickening CRUNCH.

“니타!” 엄마가 소리쳤어요. “누구 빨리 구급차를
불러주세요” 엄마는 소리치며 니타의 손을 꼭 잡고
머리를 쓰다듬었어요.
운전자는 구급차를 불렀어요.
“엄마, 다리가 아파요,” 큰 눈물방울을 떨어뜨리며 울렀어요.
“나도 안다. 아가야, 하지만 움직이면 안 된다.” 엄마가
말했어요. “구급차가 곧 올거야.”

“NITA!” Ma screamed. “Someone call an ambulance!” she shouted, stroking
Nita’s hair and holding her.
The driver dialled for an ambulance.
“Ma, my leg hurts,” cried Nita, big tears rolling down her face.
“I know it hurts, but try not to move,” said Ma. “Help will be here soon.”

RAMEDIC AMBULANCE
Surrey and Sussex NHS
AMBU
KEEP

들것을 든 두 구급요원이 도착했어요.
"안녕, 아저씨는 죤이야. 다리가 많이 부었구나. 다리가 부러진것 같은데." 구급요원이 말했어요. "아저씨가 다리 움직이지 않게 이 부목으로 묶을거야."
니타는 아랫입술을 깨물었어요. 다리가 정말 아팠어요.
"너는 정말 장한 아이야." 구급요원이 말했어요. 니타는 들것에 실려 구급차로 옮겨졌어요. 엄마도 구급차에 올랐어요.

The ambulance arrived and two paramedics came with a stretcher.
"Hello, I'm John. Your leg's very swollen. It might be broken," he said. "I'm just going to put these splints on to stop it from moving."
Nita bit her lip. The leg was really hurting.
"You're a brave girl," he said, carrying her gently on the stretcher to the ambulance. Ma climbed in too.

니타는 들것에 누워 엄마의 손을 꼭 잡고 있는 동안 구급차는 경주하듯, 도로들을 지났어요. 병원에 도착할때까지 싸이렌도 울리고 긴급등도 켰어요.

Nita lay on the stretcher holding tight to Ma, while the ambulance raced through the streets - siren wailing, lights flashing - all the way to the hospital.

병원 입구엔 이곳 저곳 사람들이 많았어요. 니타는 매우 무서웠어요.
"아가야, 어떻게 다쳤니?" 친절한 간호사가 물었어요.
"자동차에 치었는데 다리가 너무 아파요." 니타가 대답하며 눈물을 흘렸어요.
"의사 선생님이 먼저 다리를 보시고 나면, 아프지 않게 약을 줄테니 조금만 참아" 간호사는 말했어요.
"지금부터 열을 재고 피를 조금 뺄 거란다, 아주 조금 아플거야."

At the entrance there were people everywhere. Nita was feeling very scared.
"Oh dear, what's happened to you?" asked a friendly nurse.
"A car hit me and my leg really hurts," said Nita, blinking back the tears.
"We'll give you something for the pain, as soon as the doctor has had a look," he told her. "Now I've got to check your temperature and take some blood. You'll just feel a little jab."

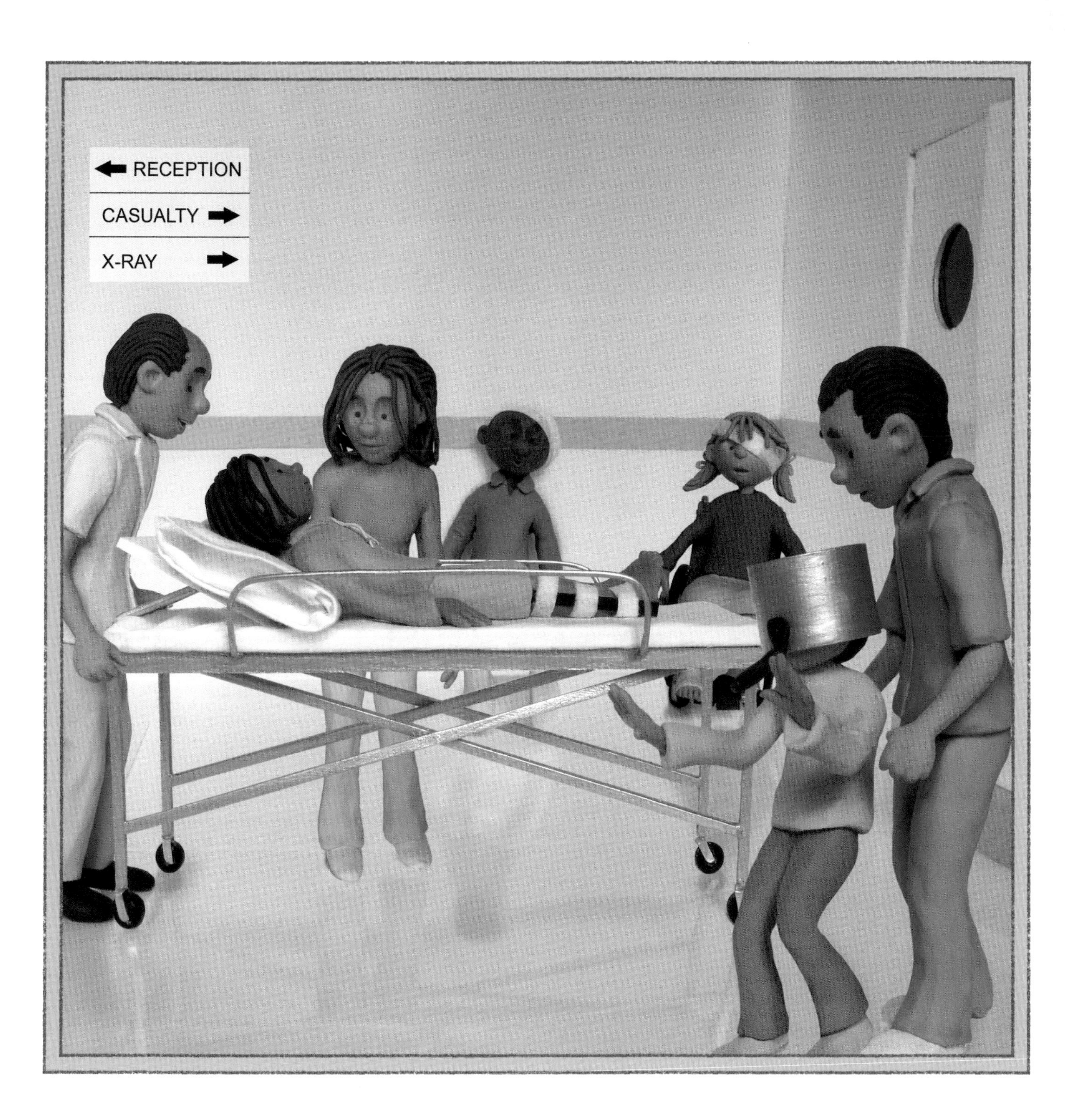
RECEPTION
CASUALTY
X-RAY

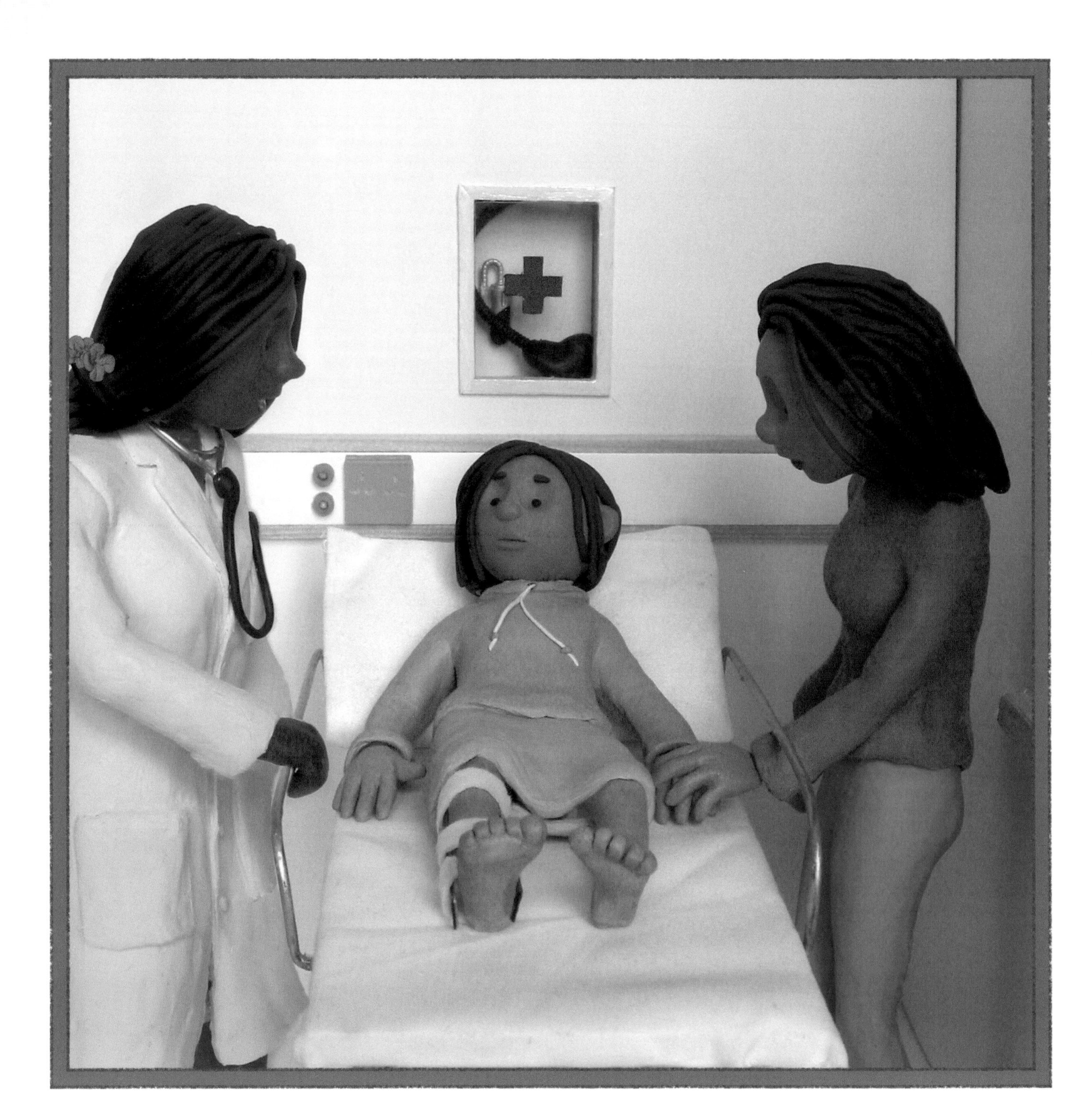

의사선생님이 도착했어요. “안녕 니타.” 의사선생님이
말했어요. “아이구, 어떻게 다친거니?”
“차에 치었는데, 다리가 많이 아파요.” 니타는 울며
대답했어요.
“내가 아프지 않게 약을 줄테니, 이제 다리를 좀 보자”
의사선생님이 말했어요. “부러진것 같구나, 우리
엑스레이를 찍어서 자세히 보자.”

Next came the doctor. “Hello Nita,” she said. “Ooh, how did that happen?”
“A car hit me. My leg really hurts,” sobbed Nita.
“I’ll give you something to stop the pain. Now let’s have a look at your leg,” said
the doctor. “Hmm, it seems broken. We’ll need an x-ray to take a closer look.”

간호보조원은 니타를 많은 사람들이 기다리고 있는
엑스레이실로 데려 갔어요.
니타의 차례가 왔어요. “안녕 니타.” 래디오그라퍼가
말했어요. “이 기계로 너의 다리속 사진을 찍을 거야.”
엑스레이기를 가리키며 그녀가 말했어요. “걱정하지마
조금도 아프지 않단다. 너는 사진을 찍을 때까지 가만히
앉아 있으면 되는 거야.”
니타는 고개를 끄덕였어요.

A friendly porter wheeled Nita to the x-ray department where lots of people
were waiting.
At last it was Nita's turn. "Hello Nita," said the radiographer. "I'm going to take a
picture of the inside of your leg with this machine," she said pointing to the x-ray
machine. "Don't worry, it won't hurt. You just have to keep very still while I take
the x-ray."
Nita nodded.

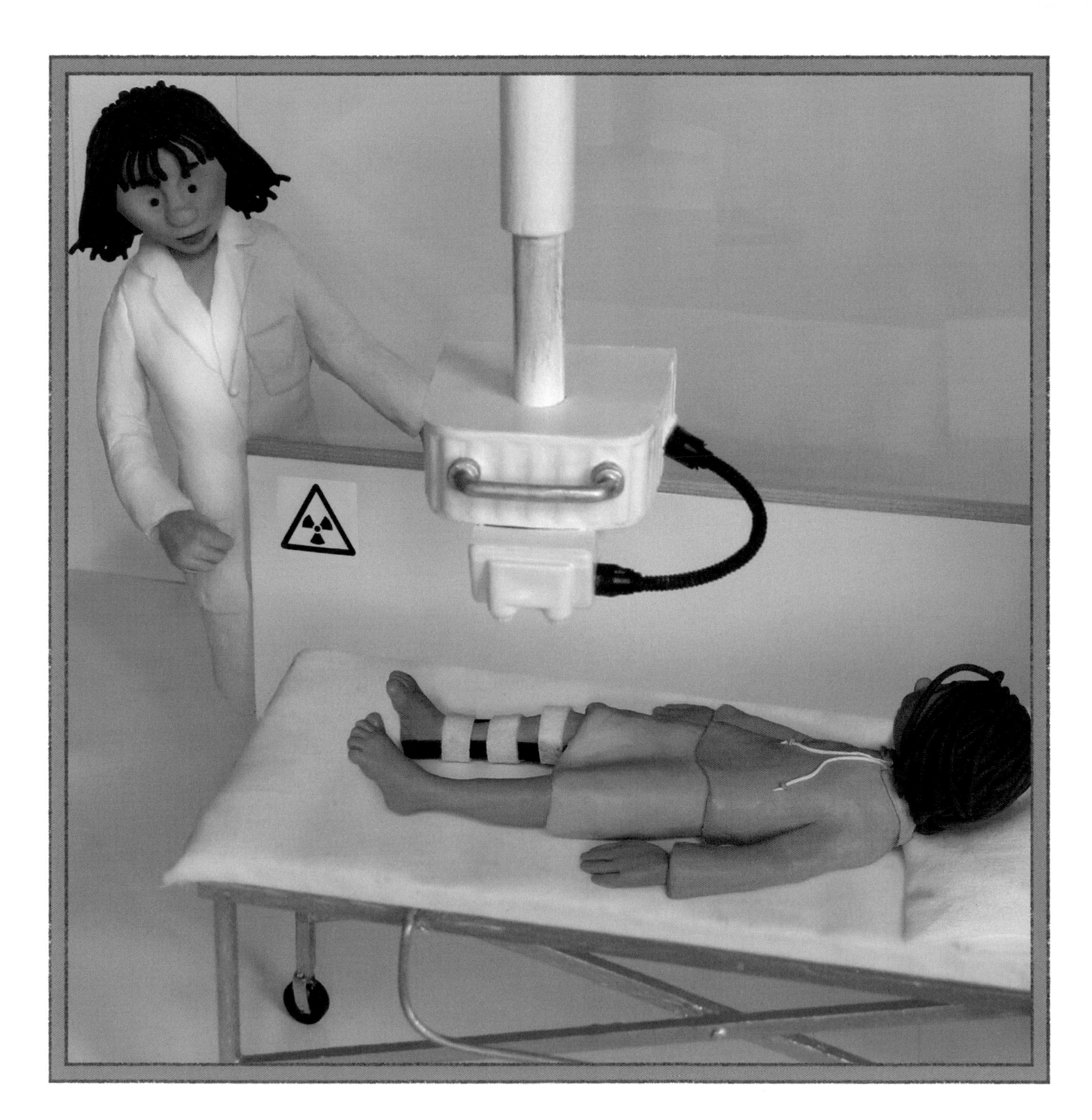

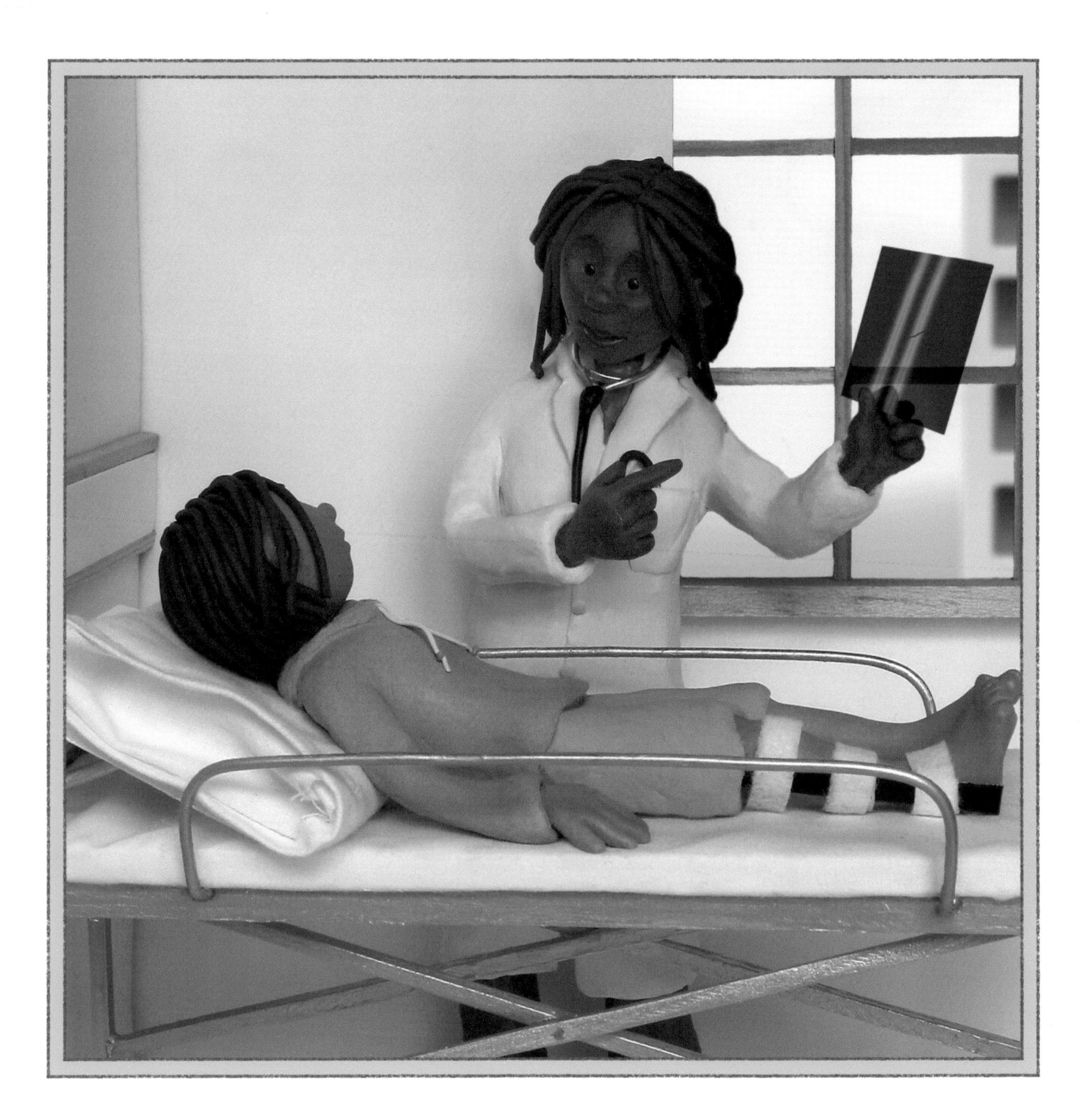

조금 후 의사선생님이 엑스레이 검사 결과를 가지고 오셨어요.
의사선생님은 니타의 다리 엑스레이사진을 보았어요.
"내가 생각했던 대로군." 의사 선생님이 말했어요. "다리가
부러졌구나, 뼈를 맞추어야 겠다, 그리고 기부스를 하면
부러진 뼈가 다시 붙을 거야, 하지만, 지금은 다리가
많이 부어 있으니, 병원에서 하룻밤 지내야 겠다. 니타야."

A little later the doctor came with the x-ray. She held it up and Nita could see the bone right inside her leg!
"It's as I thought," said the doctor. "Your leg is broken. We'll need to set it and then put on a cast. That'll hold it in place so that the bone can mend. But at the moment your leg is too swollen. You'll have to stay overnight."

간호 보조원이 니타를 어린이 병실로 데려 갔어요.
"안녕 니타. 내이름은 로즈야, 나는 너를 돌봐줄 간호사란다.
좋은 시간에 잘 맞쳐 왔구나." 간호사는 웃음을 지었어요.
"왜요?" 니타가 물었어요.
"왜냐면 저녁식사 시간이거든, 먼저 너를 침대로 옮긴 후에
저녁을 줄께."
간호사는 얼음팩을 니타의 다리에 대어주고, 다리를 받쳐줄
베게를 주었어요.

The porter wheeled Nita to the children's ward. "Hello Nita. My name's Rose and I'm your special nurse. I'll be looking after you. You've come just at the right time," she smiled.
"Why?" asked Nita.
"Because it's dinner time. We'll pop you into bed and then you can have some food."
Nurse Rose put some ice around Nita's leg and gave her an extra pillow, not for her head... but for her leg.

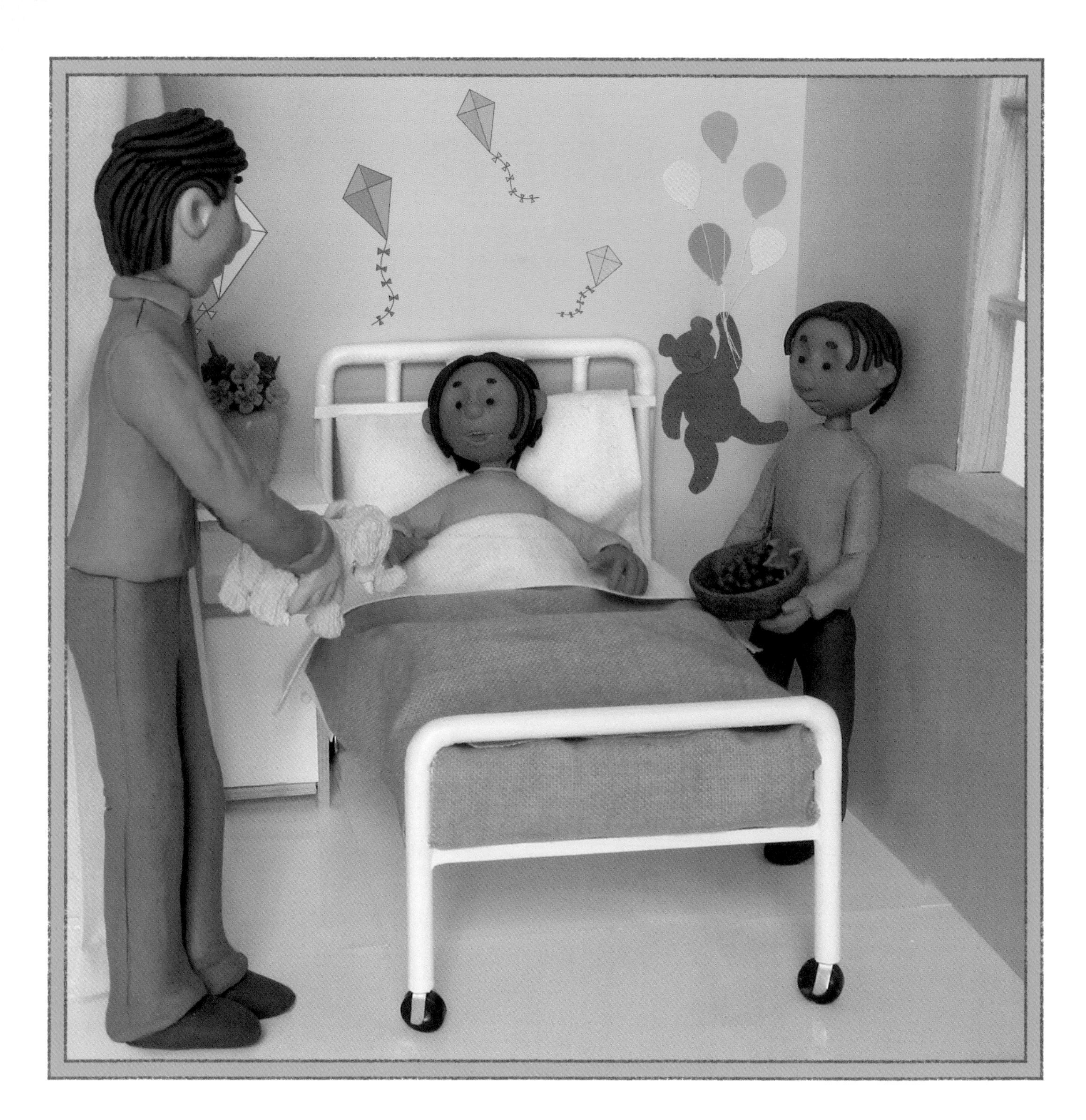

버녁 식사후, 아빠와 제이가 왔어요. 아빠는 니타를 꼭 안아주며 니타가 가장 좋아하는 장난감을 주었어요.
"다리좀 봐도 되지?" 제이가 물었어요. "으 ~ 많이 부었네. 많이 아프니?"
"아주 많이" 니타가 대답하며, "지금은 진통제를 먹어 조금은 괜찮아."
로즈 간호사는 니타의 열을 다시 쟀어요.
"이제 자야 할 시간이야, 니타." 간호사가 말했어요.
"아빠와 오빠는 집으로 돌아가야 하지만, 엄마는 오늘밤 여기 계실거야."

After dinner Dad and Jay arrived. Dad gave her a big hug and her favourite toy.
"Let's see your leg?" asked Jay. "Ugh! It's horrible. Does it hurt?"
"Lots," said Nita, "but they gave me pain-killers."
Nurse Rose took Nita's temperature again. "Time to sleep now," she said.
"Dad and your brother will have to go but Ma can stay... all night."

다음날 아침 일찍 의사선생님은 니타의 다리을 진찰 하셨어요.
"많이 좋아진 것 같구나." 의사선생님이 말했어요.
"내 생간엔, 이제 뼈를 맞추어도 되겠는걸."
"무슨 말씀인지 모르겠는데요?" 니타가 물었어요.
"선생님이 니타에게 마취제를 주면 니타는 잠을 잘거란다.
네가 자는동안, 부러진 뼈를 잘 맞추어서, 기부스를 하는
거란다. 걱정마, 하나도 아프지 않을테니." 의사선생님이
말했어요.

Early next morning the doctor checked Nita's leg. "Well that looks much better," she said. "I think it's ready to be set."
"What does that mean?" asked Nita.
"We're going to give you an anaesthetic to make you sleep. Then we'll push the bone back in the right position and hold it in place with a cast. Don't worry, you won't feel a thing," said the doctor.

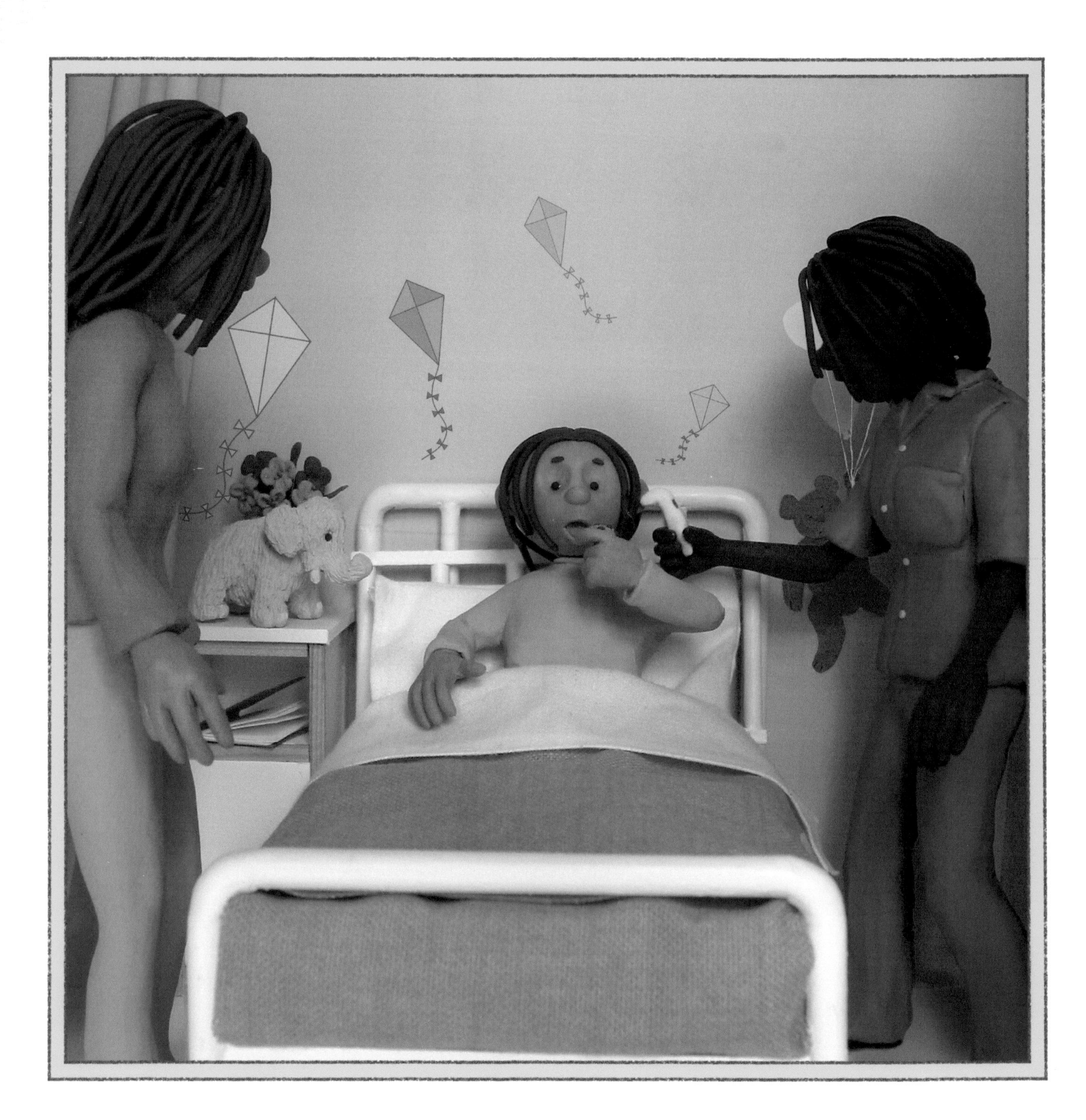

니타 생각엔, 일주일은 잔것 같았어요. "얼마나 잔거예요, 엄마?" 니타가 물었어요.
"단지, 한시간 이란다." 엄마는 웃음을 지었어요.
"안녕 니타." 로즈 간호사가 말했어요. "잠에서 깨어나 반갑다. 다리는 좀 어때?"
"괜찮아요. 하지만, 무겁고 불편해요." 니타가 말했어요. "뭐 먹을 것 좀 주실래요?"
"그래. 곧 점심시간 이야." 로즈 간호사가 말했어요.

Nita felt like she'd been asleep for a whole week. "How long have I been sleeping, Ma?" she asked.
"Only about an hour," smiled Ma.
"Hello Nita," said Nurse Rose. "Good to see you've woken up. How's the leg?"
"OK, but it feels so heavy and stiff," said Nita. "Can I have something to eat?"
"Yes, it'll be lunchtime soon," said Rose.

점심후엔, 니타의 기분이 더 좋아졌어요. 로즈 간호사는 니타를 휠체어에 태워, 다른 친구들과 놀수 있게 해 주었어요.
“어디를 다쳤니?” 한 소년이 물었어요.
“다리가 부러졌어.” 니타가 대답했어요. “너는?”
“나는 귀가 아파, 수술을 했어.” 소년이 대답했어요.

By lunchtime Nita was feeling much better. Nurse Rose put her in a wheelchair so that she could join the other children.
“What happened to you?” asked a boy.
“Broke my leg,” said Nita. “And you?”
“I had an operation on my ears,” said the boy.

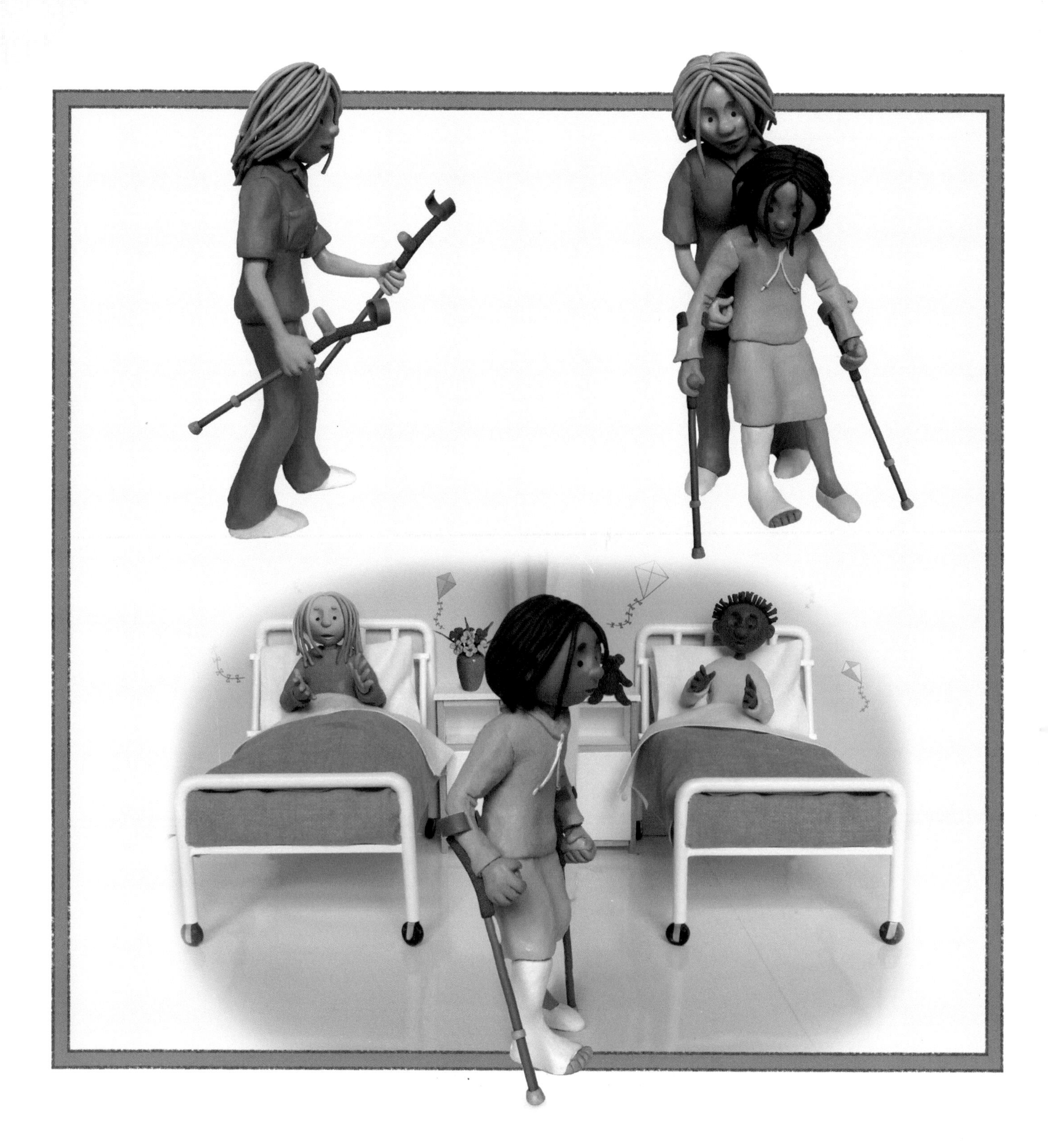

오후엔, 물리치료사가 목발을 가지고 왔어요.
"여기 있다. 니타야. 이 목발이 움직이는데, 도움이 될거야,"
물리치료사가 말했어요.
기우뚱 기우뚱, 쩔뚝 쩔뚝, 니타는 곧 병실을 돌아 다닐 수
있게 되었어요.
"잘 하는구나." 물리치료사가 말했어요. "내 생각엔, 이제
집에 가도 되겠다. 내가 의사 선생님을 모셔 올께."

In the afternoon the physiotherapist came with some crutches. "Here you are Nita. These will help you to get around," she said.
Hobbling and wobbling, pushing and holding, Nita was soon walking around the ward.
"Well done," said the physiotherapist. "I think you're ready to go home. I'll get the doctor to see you."

그날 저녁, 엄마 아빠 그리고, 록키가 니타를 데리러 왔어요.
"볼만한데." 제이가 니타의 기부스를 보며 말했어요.
"내가 기브스 위에 그림 그려도 돼?"
"지금은 않돼 오빠! 집에 가서 해." 니타가 말했어요.
기부스를 하는 것이, 그렇게 나쁜 것만은 아니었어요.

That evening Ma, Dad, Jay and Rocky came to collect Nita.
"Cool," said Jay seeing Nita's cast. "Can I draw on it?"
"Not now! When we get home," said Nita. Maybe having a cast wasn't going to be so bad.